TALES TOO G█████████████████ E

The Chicken-Fried RAT

By Cylin Busby

Illustrated by
Phoebe Gloeckner and Ravenblond Studios

Introduction by Jan Harold Brunvand

HarperTrophy®
A Division of HarperCollins*Publishers*

Don't Miss These Tales Too Outrageous To Be True:

The Baby-Sitter's Nightmare:
Tales Too Scary to Be True

The Exploding Toilet:
Tales Too Funny to Be True

To all the kids who told me their "true" stories
and for Jan Harold Brunvand and Alan Dundes.
—C.B.

Many thanks to A. Suits, F. Gloeckner-Kalousek,
and especially P. Mavrides.
—P.G.

Harper Trophy® is a registered trademark of HarperCollins Publishers Inc.

The Chicken-Fried Rat
Text copyright © 1998 by Cylin Busby
Illustrations copyright © 1998 by Phoebe Gloeckner

Library of Congress Cataloging-in-Publication Data
Busby, Cylin.
  The chicken-fried rat : tales too gross to be true / by Cylin Busby ; illustrated by Phoebe Gloeckner.
    p.   cm.
  Summary: Eric and his friends spend a day sharing disgusting, supposedly true stories, including ones about eyeball juice at midnight, a baby in an oven, and the chicken-fried rat. Features an introduction discussing the phenomenon of urban legends.
  ISBN 0-06-440701-2
  [1. Horror stories.   2. Urban folklore.]   I. Gloeckner, Phoebe, ill.
II. Title.
PZ7.B9556Ch 1998   98-8051
[Fic]—dc21   CIP
                                               AC

1 2 3 4 5 6 7 8 9 10

First Edition

Contents

Introduction
by Jan Harold Brunvand

The gross stories that Eric Alward, his friends, and family tell in this book are known as *urban legends*. *Legends*, because they are unlikely and unprovable stories, told as if they were true; *urban*, because they deal with everyday life in modern cities and suburbs.

Some people call these weird stories *urban myths*, while others use the term *contemporary legends*. Whatever they're called, they are definitely not *jokes*, which are funny stories that nobody really believes. Nor are they one-hundred-percent true stories, even though there are some elements of truth in even the weirdest urban legend.

When you consider that the same urban legends are told all over the United States—and even in some foreign countries—it becomes pretty obvious that they cannot all be true. And when you look at all the coincidences and the lack of specific details in the stories, you realize that probably none of the stories are really true.

People often say that the incidents in urban legends happened to a friend of a friend; people who study urban legends call this supposed source a FOAF. The source of the story is never firsthand, but always one or two friends removed from the teller. Another thing that makes urban legends seem plausible is that they deal with familiar topics, like fast food, tanning salons, house plants, and pets.

Urban legends are part of folklore, and people who collect and study folklore are called folklorists. Although other folklorists like to study old songs and ballads, fairy tales, superstitions, customs, and so on, my own special topic is urban legends. I've been collecting them for about forty years, and I've published five books about them, each one titled after a famous urban legend: *The Vanishing Hitchhiker* (1981), *The Choking Doberman* (1984), *The Mexican Pet* (1986), *Curses! Broiled Again!* (1989), and *The Baby Train* (1993). Maybe you've heard some of the urban legends referred to in these titles. (Hint:

One of them is retold in this very book.)

The first urban legend I remember hearing, sometime during high school, was a gross one about the Death Car. It was about an expensive late-model car supposedly for sale at a local dealer at a very low price. A deer hunter had died in the car when he was parked way out in the woods, and the police didn't find his body until it had badly decomposed.

The car dealer was unable to get rid of the stench from the decaying corpse, so he was offering to sell the car, a Buick, for $50. As I continued to study folklore, I found the same story told about different models of cars whose drivers had died in different ways and that were on sale for different prices. Most recently it was a vintage Corvette sold for $500. I never found—or smelled—the legendary death car itself.

Variations are what define all kinds of folklore, so if you haven't heard the very same version of a story as the one presented in this book, you may have heard a retelling of it with different details. Folklorists call this kind of story a variant.

How does someone become a folklorist? Like people with jobs in many other fields, you go to college and study the subject. I went to Indiana University, where there's a world-famous program in folklore, and after writing a thesis and graduating with a Ph.D. in folklore (this is true!) I became a teacher and researcher on the subject. Eventually I narrowed my topic to urban legends because I found it fascinating to study a kind of folk story that was still being made up and retold from person to person. Living folklore, you might call it.

And I'm not alone anymore. The International Society for Contemporary Legend Research (ISCLR) was founded in 1988, and when this group published a bibliography of urban legend publications in 1993, the book had 1,116 entries! So there's plenty more to read about urban legends if you are interested in going beyond the stories in this book and the two others that accompany it.

Jan Harold Brunvand is a professor emeritus of English and folklore at the University of Utah.

Chapter 1

The Chicken-Fried Rat

Eric Alward woke with a start and grabbed his alarm clock. Eight-thirty! He was late, very late for school. Why hadn't the alarm gone off? Why hadn't his mom woken him?

Then it hit him: Because it was June 7, otherwise known as the first day of summer vacation. Eric lay down again, but it was no use trying to sleep. He was wide awake. And besides, he had a very busy summer ahead of him.

He stumbled into the kitchen and found a box of Fudge-Os in the cabinet. His mom usually wouldn't buy them—she claimed that sugar-coated cereal caused cavities and hyperactivity, whatever that was. But when his mom started working a few months ago, the grocery shopping became Eric's job. These days, there were usually a few boxes of Fudge-Os in the cabinet.

Eric poured the cereal into a bowl, then walked over to the refrigerator for some milk. And that's when he saw it: The List. One of his mother's famous To Do lists. With his name written right across the top in big capital letters. *Doesn't she know it's the first day of summer vacation*? thought Eric. He yanked the list down, grabbed the milk, and tried to enjoy his Fudge-Os. That's when he got his second bad surprise of the day: There, right in the middle of his cereal, was a big blue blob. "Ugh!" he exclaimed. "What's that?"

"What's what?" asked Eric's brother as he walked into the kitchen.

"*That!*" Eric pointed to the blue thing floating in his bowl.

"Oh . . . that, my friend, is none other than a Super Secret Fudge-O Decoder Bracelet." Shawn scooped the blue plastic blob out of the milk. "Finders keepers," he sang out as he dried the band and strapped it onto his wrist.

"Don't you think fifteen is a little old to be wearing some dorky decoder?" Eric asked him. "*I* wouldn't even wear that stupid thing.

It's for a kindergartner or something."

"It's kitsch, man," said Shawn. "Kitsch is, like, beyond cool. And forget kindergartners. You can't even eat breakfast without throwing a fit." Shawn started dancing from foot to foot, making fun of Eric. "'Oh no! What's that in my cereal? Ah! Help me, help me!' You'd think you just ate the Chicken-Fried Rat or something."

"The Chicken-Fried *what*?" asked Eric, his mouth full of soggy Fudge-Os.

"You really are the lamest," Shawn said, pulling up a chair. He sat down and leaned back, his arms across his chest, while carefully balancing the chair on its two back legs. "Have I ever told you how lucky you are to have me as your brother?" he asked, tossing a lock of hair out of his eyes.

"Yeah," Eric mumbled. "But only every day, twice a day."

"Okay then, because I'm your big bro, and I take pity on a little loser like you, I'll tell you about the Chicken-Fried Rat. Remember that kid Mark whose mom owned the Kwik-ee Mart on Tenth Street? Well, his cousin from Connecticut told him this story. . . ."

There was a teenage couple who were on their way to the prom. The girl was in a really fancy dress, and the guy was in a tuxedo. They thought it would be fun to go to a fast-food restaurant dressed up like that and have everyone wonder where they were going. So they drove to the local fried-chicken place, and just as they had planned, they made quite a scene as they waltzed in and ordered their food. There were no tables left inside, so the couple decided to eat in the car. They loved having every eye on them as they left the restaurant—it was so cool. They couldn't wait to tell their friends what they'd done.

The guy drove to a romantic overlook nearby, where they could eat. Night was falling, so they had a great view of the city lights as they started in on their dinner of fried chicken, mashed potatoes, and coleslaw. The guy bit into a chicken wing. "Mmmmm, yum!" he said. His girlfriend helped herself to a drumstick. The guy finished off another wing and said, "This stuff is good, but it's awful greasy. Can you pass me a napkin?"

"That's funny," said the girl. "My piece isn't greasy at all." She looked around for a napkin, but she couldn't find one in the dark car, so she turned on the overhead light.

That's when she saw a long, dark tail was sticking out of her drumstick.

Gagging, she spat out what was in her mouth. It was a deep-fried rat, covered in dark, bristly hair!

The girl fainted dead away, and her boyfriend had no idea what to do. He decided to pour his soda over her head to revive her. It worked—but when she came to, she was drenched in sticky root beer. Then she remembered what she had just been chewing and started to throw up—all over the car, all over her date, and all over herself. This didn't do very much for her prom dress.

Her boyfriend drove straight to the hospital. The doctors there looked at the half-eaten deep-fried rat and decided they would have to pump her stomach. I guess you could say that ended any plans they had for going to the prom.

The girl's family decided to sue the fast-food restaurant for serving her a fried rat. They had no problem finding witnesses to testify that they had seen the couple buying dinner there. Who could forget the sight of the prom couple who waltzed in that night as if they owned the place? . . .

Eric stared down at his Fudge-Os and wondered what else might be lurking in the murky depths of his cereal bowl. "Is that *really* a true story?" he asked.

"Every word of it," Shawn said. "Hey, you gonna eat those Fudge-Os? You finished the last box of cereal, you know."

"I'm not hungry anymore." Eric pushed the bowl of cereal over to his brother. "Here, you can have it," he said. "I'm outta here."

As Eric left, Shawn dug into the heaping bowl and started shoveling Fudge-Os into his mouth. "Works every time!" he said, grinning as a little bit of fudge-colored milk dribbled down his chin.

Chapter 2

The Mixed-Up Baby-Sitter

As soon as Eric stepped outside into the bright sunshine, he felt better. After all, it was almost summer. The air smelled of freshly cut grass; across the street, Mr. Johnson was mowing his lawn; and next door, the Anderson twins and their baby-sitter were washing the family car.

"Hi, Eric!" one of the twins called out. "Hi, Eric!" the other twin called out. Their baby-sitter smiled and waved too. The twins were just a year younger than Eric, but they still had a baby-sitter. Eric was glad his parents didn't think he needed a baby-sitter anymore—they just left him with Shawn during the day. *Good thing they don't know what a pain Shawn can be*, thought Eric. If they did, he'd still have to deal with a baby-sitter. That would be so embarrassing.

He decided to get busy with his mom's To

Do list and forget about Shawn for the rest of the day. The first thing on the list was a trip to the hardware store for something called a poultry timer. So Eric made his way down the block to Main Street and Mr. Flynn's hardware store.

Mr. Flynn was old—very, very old. Nobody knew what his age was, but most of the kids thought he had to be at least a hundred. Eric hated to go to Mr. Flynn's alone because the old man was forever lecturing the neighborhood kids. He always thought everyone was shoplifting. Whenever kids were in the store, Mr. Flynn would follow them around, saying, "You gonna buy that?" and "Don't touch it unless you wanna pay for it!"

Eric pushed open the door, and a little bell tinkled. He decided to get the timer his mom wanted and be out of there—fast—before Mr. Flynn had a chance to give him a hard time. Eric made his way over to the cookware aisle. His mom had written *poultry timer with pop-up button*. What did that mean? Eric looked up and down the shelves. Nothing in the dusty old shop was labeled, and all the pans and cooking equipment were just jumbled together. He was sure that if he touched one item, the whole pile of stuff would come tumbling down on his head.

Just as he was looking behind some pots, he heard a loud, scratchy voice. "Don't touch it unless you wanna pay for it, sonny!" called old Mr. Flynn, making his way down the aisle with his cane. He wobbled this way and that as he came toward Eric, then held out his cane, shaking it in Eric's face. "You kids! Always in here! Always stealing things from me! You think I'm so old that I don't know what's going on? I know; I see you kids!" He finally stopped shaking the cane, but from behind his thick spectacles he continued to glare at Eric.

I shouldn't have come to Mr. Flynn's alone, thought Eric. *Why didn't I get Tom to come with me?* "Uh, my mom sent me here to get a poultry timer . . . with a pop-up button," he mumbled.

The old man kept glaring at him. "Oh yeah? Is that so? You expect me to believe

10

that? Why, you're hardly old enough to be out of diapers! Your mother wouldn't send you out alone! And shouldn't you be at school? A truant, and a thief! I oughta report you to the police!"

"Mr. Flynn," Eric tried again, "it's summer vacation. That's why I'm not at school. And my mom really did send me here. Look at the list she gave me." Eric held it out so Mr. Flynn could see it. The old man peered at it.

"Well, I can hardly believe it! What kind of a mother would send a little child out all alone like this! It's just not right, the way these modern mothers are! Let me tell you something, sonny, back in my day . . ."

Oh no! Eric cringed. Every time old Mr. Flynn launched into one of his long-winded stories, he started with the same phrase: *"Back in my day . . ."*

". . . a family would raise their own children," Mr. Flynn continued. "We didn't have any of these newfangled baby-sitter types. Nobody would ever think of paying somebody else to do the raising for them.

11

Nothing but trouble there, I'll tell you. Baby-sitters! They're hardly more than babies themselves! You have a baby-sitter, sonny?"

"No," Eric responded weakly. "I really need to find this poultry timer thing and get to my swimming lesson, though—"

"Well, you're better off without a baby-sitter, considering. You're probably too young to remember all that trouble we had back in 'seventy-seven with that young lady. . . . Now, why can't I remember her name? Well, doesn't matter now, because she ended up in jail after what she did—serves her right, too, putting that innocent little baby into the oven like that—"

"What?" Eric interrupted. "Who put a baby in an oven?"

Old Mr. Flynn leaned forward on his cane. There was a wicked sparkle in his eyes as he looked Eric up and down. "Some might think that this story is a little bit too gruesome for a young tyke like you, but I'll tell it to you—for your own good. . . ."

There was a young lady hereabouts, looking to make a little extra money one summer. She tried a few odd jobs, but she always got fired after a few days because she was so forgetful. Even the simplest tasks took her forever. So she checked in the Help Wanted ads of the local paper and read that someone in her neighborhood needed a baby-sitter. Looking after children seemed easy enough, so she decided to take the job.

She went over to the family's house that Saturday to watch their six-month-old baby while they went out for the evening. The little boy was just as cute as a button, and the girl was sure the job would be very simple.

Just before the couple left, the mother said, "Could you do me a favor and put this roast in the oven tonight? We're having guests over for lunch tomorrow, and it needs to cook for a long time." The girl said she wouldn't mind at all. So the mother gave her the directions for the roast, and for the baby, and then left for the evening.

The baby-sitter repeated the mother's directions: "Put the roast in the oven at eight-thirty at three hundred and fifty degrees. Put the baby in the bassinet at eight o'clock sharp, with a bottle of milk that's been warmed to seventy-five degrees."

But after the parents left, the baby-sitter just couldn't keep the directions straight. She kept repeating them over and over to herself, hoping that she'd get them right. "Put the roast in the oven at seventy-five degrees at eight o'clock sharp. Put the baby in the bassinet at eight-thirty, with a bottle of milk that has been warmed to three hundred and fifty degrees." No, no, that wasn't it! "Put the baby in the oven at eight-thirty at seventy-five degrees, put the roast in the bassinet at eight o'clock sharp with a bottle of milk at three hundred and fifty degrees." Was that it?

The girl tried very hard, but there were so many numbers and times and temperatures to keep track of! She'd just have to do her best. . . .

A few hours later, the parents came home. The house was warm, the oven was on, but where was the baby-sitter? The mother checked the dial on the stove and

saw that the temperature was set, just as she had asked, at 350 degrees. And the timer had been set at 8:30, which was also right. The mother was very pleased. Then she went to check on the baby. She saw a little bundle in the bassinet, all wrapped up, and tiptoed over so she wouldn't wake the sleeping infant. But when she arranged the blanket, she got the shock of her life: There was the roast—wrapped up in a blanket in the baby's bassinet!

How strange! the mother thought. *I wonder where my baby is?* And then she had a terrible thought. If the *roast* was in the *baby's* crib, then what was cooking in the oven? Just then the baby-sitter walked into the room. "Oh, you're home!" she said. "I was just about to check on the baby." Then she walked into the kitchen and opened the oven door. There, in a big pan, was the little baby. It had been cooking for hours. . . .

"That's the most horrible thing I've ever heard!" Eric said. "I can't believe it!"

"It's true," said Mr. Flynn, cackling. "But

look at me, carrying on here when you've got things to do. Now, let's see—you say you need a poultry timer, eh? Looks like we got it right here, sonny." Mr. Flynn held out what looked like a small metal thermometer. "You just tell your mom to stick that right into her chicken before she puts it in the oven. And you can tell your baby-sitter it's good for cooking little boys, too." The old man winked as he handed Eric the timer.

Chapter 3

Broiled Alive!

After paying Mr. Flynn, Eric ran all the way to the pool, but he was still a few minutes late. As he ran up the steps to the pool deck, a lifeguard hollered, "Hey, you! No running by the pool!" Eric stopped short, almost tripping over two girls lying in the sun.

"Watch it! You're blocking our sun!" said one of them. Eric looked down. The two girls were Polly and Nanci, his friends from school. And he was casting a shadow on them.

"Sorry," he said, moving out of the way so that the sun could shine down on them. Just then, a lifeguard called out, "Pee-Wee swimmers, line up for lessons at the shallow end!"

"Pee-Wee!" Eric looked at his watch. It was eleven A.M. "I thought it was time for *my* swimming lesson."

"Nope," Polly said. "You're taking lessons with Tom, right? Your class was at ten."

"Are you sure? I thought it was at eleven," Eric said.

"Polly's right," said Nanci. "Tom was here at ten, and he was looking all over for you. We've been here since nine this morning working on our tans. Can you believe it's the first day of summer vacation, and here we are, pale as ghosts!"

The girls did look pale to Eric. Then he noticed that they were both wearing matching bathing suits—white with little red polka dots. "Hey," he said. "Did you guys know you both have on the same bathing suit?"

"Gee, what a surprise," said Polly sarcastically.

Nanci had always been the nicer of the two girls. "It took us weeks to find matching suits in our sizes," she said. "What do you think?"

"I think they're great," Eric said. "They'd look even better with a tan." As soon as the words were out of his mouth, Eric knew he'd said the wrong thing.

"Well, that was exactly what we were trying to do before *you* showed up!" Polly snapped.

"Don't mind her," Nanci said. "She's just mad because her mom won't let her go to the tanning booth to get a fake tan."

"A fake tan? What's that?" asked Eric.

"You know," Nanci said. "A tan in a tanning booth, where they shine those ultraviolet lights on you and make you look like you've been in the sun. You can even go there in the winter and get a tan—it's great!"

"Or not so great," Polly added.

"Oh, yeah, I keep forgetting," Nanci said.

"Forgetting what?" Eric asked.

"Well, we heard a story about this girl. . . ."

It was just a few weeks before the Spring Fling—the most important dance of the school year—and Candy, the most popular girl in school, still hadn't found the perfect dress. She had to look incredible for the dance, because she was sure this was her year to be voted Queen of the Spring Fling.

So she tried on dress after dress, but none of them was truly spectacular. Then, just five days before the dance, Candy tried on the dress of her dreams. It was creamy white silk, the color of vanilla ice cream, and it fit her as if it had been made for her. Candy didn't care how expensive it was—she just had to have it.

After she bought her dress, Candy realized she still had a lot to do before the Fling. She had to find matching shoes. She had to get her hair done and get a manicure. And most important, she had to get a tan. Only a tan would make her look sensational enough to be Queen of the Fling.

So Candy found a tanning salon and started going there every day. She spent hours and hours baking under the ultraviolet lights. The people at the salon warned her against overdoing it, but Candy didn't listen to them. She wanted a really deep tan. And by the day of the Fling, she had one.

That night, Candy was a vision in her new dress. Her skin was a deep tropical brown, and no one at the dance looked more beautiful. Her boyfriend, however, was not happy. Something about Candy was different, and it wasn't just her tan. "You smell funny!" he said as they were dancing.

"What do you mean?" she asked.

"You smell like burned meat!" he said, wrinkling his nose.

Candy was so mad, she stormed off to the ladies' room. Once she was inside a stall, she sniffed her arm. It did smell a little strange. Then she sniffed her hand. That smelled strange too. She really wanted to go home and take a shower, but it was too late; it was almost time for the coronation of the king and queen of the dance. By the time Candy made her way back out to the dance floor, she was feeling light-headed. That smell was really starting to bother her. What could it be?

She scanned the crowd, looking around for her boyfriend, but she couldn't find him. And now she felt worse: Her head ached, and so did her stomach.

Maybe I should go home, she thought. But just then the class president took the stage

to announce the winners. To her horror, someone else's name was called for Queen of the Spring Fling! After all that hard work, and all those hours tanning, she hadn't even won! She was so upset, and felt so sick, that she passed out right on the dance floor.

When Candy awoke, she was in a hospital bed. Her mother and father were there, and so was her boyfriend. "Candy," said her boyfriend, "I'm so sorry I left you at the dance by yourself. I never should have done that." Candy was about to forgive him, when she suddenly remembered the contest. "I can't believe I didn't win Queen of the Spring Fling!" she cried. Tears ran down her face, and she sniffled a little as she asked, "But why am I in the hospital? I'm not sick, am I?"

Candy's mother starting sobbing.

"What is it, Mom?" Candy asked. "What's the matter?"

"We'd better let the doctor explain it to you," said her father, with tears in his eyes. A doctor came in and asked everyone to leave for a moment. When he was alone with

Candy, he asked, "Have you been going to a tanning salon?"

"Sure," she answered. "Why do you ask?"

"I'm afraid I have some bad news for you," said the doctor. "You spent too many hours under those intense lights. I'm sorry, but your internal organs have been . . . well, they've been *cooked* by the ultraviolet lights. You've virtually been baked, from the inside out. And now you have only about a week to live. . . ."

"I can't believe that!" Eric said. "Did that *really* happen?"

"Yup," Polly answered. "My cousin's best friend's sister is the one who told me, and I guess she would know."

"Yech!" Eric said. "That's one of the grossest things I've ever heard!"

Nanci sat up and started rubbing herself with tanning lotion. "Now you can see why we prefer a *natural* tan!" she said.

Chapter 4

Shake 'n Bake Poodle

"**H**ey, Eric!" called a voice from the pool snack bar. It was Tom, Eric's best friend. Dressed in swim trunks, he had a towel over his shoulder and a camera around his neck. Tom had decided in third grade that he was going to be a photographer. He already had a mini-darkroom set up in his basement and he never went out without his camera.

As Tom made his way over to Eric, Polly, and Nanci, he lifted the camera to his eye. "Stay right there—don't move!" He snapped a quick picture before joining his friends. "So, where were you this morning?" he asked Eric. "I called your house, but Shawn said you'd already left."

"It's a long story," Eric sighed. "Hey, Tom, have you ever heard about the girl who went to a tanning booth and got her insides cooked?"

"Sure," said Tom. "Everybody knows that story. Which reminds me—have you heard the one about the crazy old lady who tried to dry her poodle in the microwave?"

"Ewwwwww!" Polly squealed. "What happened?"

"Well," Tom began, "the way I heard it . . ."

There was this little old lady who lived all by herself. Her only friend was her tiny poodle. Since she didn't have any family, she treated that dog like he was her child; she bought him toys and treats, and bathed and trimmed him once a week, so he always looked like a show dog.

Then one day the little old lady won a prize in a magazine contest—a brand-new microwave oven. Well, she'd never owned a microwave before, so she was very excited. The oven was delivered and installed, and the old lady starting using it right away. She boiled a cup of tea in it. Then she heated up a bowl of soup. Then she defrosted some chicken. She was really happy with the new addition to her kitchen. It was going to make her life a lot easier.

It just so happened that the day the oven came, Wednesday, was the day her poodle usually got his bath. So she ran Fluffy's bathwater, added his special bubble bath, and plopped him in. After a good scrubbing, she took him out of the tub and dried him with a towel. She usually used the hair dryer on Fluffy to make sure his fur got nice and poofy as it dried. But today she had a much better idea: Why not put him in the microwave? It would be warm and cozy, and she could put the oven on a low setting, just right for drying fur.

So she took the little dog into the kitchen and stuffed him into the microwave. He started yapping and barking and trying to scratch his way out. "Just be quiet for one minute, Fluffy," the little old lady told him. She remembered how fast the microwave had boiled her cup of tea, so she set the timer for just two minutes. "This won't take very long," she said to the little dog. Then she turned the oven on and watched

the poodle through the glass door.

First his fur stood on end. Then he started barking and squirming, and his little eyes started to bulge out. The next thing the old lady knew, the microwave exploded, splattering her precious poodle all over the kitchen. . . .

Chapter 5

The Bubbling Belly

"**I** don't know why, but suddenly I'm just dying for a hot dog," announced Tom. "How about you guys?"

Nanci and Polly screamed "*Ewwwwww!*" at the same time.

"I wouldn't mind a *hot* dog myself . . . with mustard and relish!" Eric agreed, laughing.

"You guys are *sooo* gross," Polly said, scowling.

"Come on, let's head over to the Kwik-ee Mart," Nanci said. "My mom just gave me my allowance this morning. We can get our first slushees of the summer!"

"Yeah!" Tom chimed in. "I'm gonna get a Blueberry Freeze—no, make that a Purple Punch Pucker! Let's go!"

"Oh, all right," Polly grumbled, picking up her towel. "But I hope you guys realize that we're missing the prime suntanning hours."

As they walked over, Tom kept trying to decide what flavor slushee he was going to get. "I love that Strawberry Swirl they had last summer, but then again, there's my old favorite, Gooberlicious Grape."

The kids were practically drooling by the time they reached the convenience store. There was a microwave right next to the slushee machine.

"Hey, Eric," called Tom. "Here's a great new way to dry your hair after swimming lessons." He stuck his head into the oven. "Ruff-ruff!" he barked.

Nanci and Eric laughed, but Polly just shook her head in disgust. "Grow up, Tom. Sometimes I cannot believe that you're going into sixth grade next year." She grabbed a big plastic cup and starting filling it with Blueberry Freeze from the slushee machine.

"I'm next!" Nanci called out. She grabbed a big cup and filled it with Raspberry Royal Ice. "Did you decide, Tom?"

"Yes, I have finally reached a decision,"

Tom said. "It'll be the Gooberlicious Grape today, and tomorrow I'll have my other favorite, the Strawberry Swirl."

Eric was busy getting a soda and some candy. "How can you guys drink those things? They're so cold, they always give me a head freeze."

"You just have to drink it slo-o-o-o-owly—or be man enough to put up with the pain," Tom explained, taking a big gulp of his icy purple drink.

They all gathered at the counter, piling their slushees and snacks in front of the cashier so he could ring everything up.

"Hey, man," the clerk said, pointing at Eric. "Aren't you Shawn Alward's little brother?"

"Yeah," Eric mumbled.

"I was in study hall with him. He's one funny dude! How's he doing?"

"Fine," Eric said, grimacing. He hated being recognized as Shawn's little brother. People always expected him to be like Shawn.

"Hey, who's getting the Sweet Fizz?" the

clerk asked, holding up the packet of candy. Sweet Fizz came in a little packet, like sugar, and it looked like sugar too. When you put it in your mouth, it started to fizz and pop. It was Eric's favorite candy.

"Um, that's mine," he said.

The clerk held up Eric's bottle of soda. "Let me give you some advice," he said. "Don't ever drink soda and eat Sweet Fizz at the same time, or you'll be sorry—*very* sorry!"

"Why?" Polly asked, raising her eyebrows.

"You guys never heard about what happened to Mikey?" The clerk looked at them in disbelief.

"Who's Mikey?" asked Tom.

"You know, *Mikey*, from the cereal commercial . . ." said the clerk.

The kids just looked at each other. They had no idea what the clerk was talking about.

"Maybe you guys are too young to know this story," the clerk said. "But I'd better tell it to you—before you go and do something stupid. There was this kid actor. . . ."

✳ ✳ ✳ ✳ ✳

His name was Mikey—or at least that was his name in the cereal commercial that made him famous. Mikey was an adorable little redheaded, freckle-faced kid. You know, the kind of kid that parents just love. He was so adorable that he was cast for this cereal commercial, and suddenly everyone in America loved him.

Unfortunately, the fame went straight to Mikey's head. Right after he did the cereal ad, Mikey started disobeying his parents, and throwing temper tantrums when he didn't get his way. He wouldn't go to bed on time, he wouldn't eat his veggies at dinner, and he started skipping school.

One day, Mikey was in the grocery store with his mom. He wanted junk food, soda and candy and stuff, and his mom wouldn't get it for him. So he started to scream at her.

"Do you know who I am?" he shouted. "I'm *Mikey*! America loves me! And you won't even let me have one can of pop?"

So finally his mom gave in. She bought

him all the candy he wanted, which was every single flavor of Sweet Fizz, and a huge bottle of soda. He started guzzling it all down at once, before they'd even left the store. He'd eat handfuls of Sweet Fizz, take a big gulp of soda, eat more Sweet Fizz, and drink more soda.

By the time they reached the car, Mikey had started to feel funny.

"My stomach's burning," he whined.

"I'm sure it is," his mom said, "with all the junk you're eating."

Mikey ate another packet of Sweet Fizz and took one last big gulp of soda before climbing into the car. "Ugh," he said, holding his stomach. "My stomach *really* feels funny!"

"Well, stop eating that stuff!" said his mom. "And buckle your seatbelt, or we're not going anywhere."

Mikey tried to yank the seatbelt over his waist. "I can't!" he said. "Look at my stomach!" His belly was as round as a beach ball. "Mom! Make it stop!" cried Mikey as the candy and soda rumbled and bubbled and churned in his stomach.

"Owwwwww," he cried, holding his ever-expanding belly. "Owwwww." Just when he looked like he was about to pop, a frothy stream of Sweet Fizz bubbles came out of his mouth.

Mikey's mom was horrified! Mikey tried to say something else, but more Sweet Fizz came bubbling out of his mouth.

And then . . . his stomach completely exploded! The bubbling action from the candy, combined with the gas from the soda, created a lethal belly bomb.

Chapter 6

Eyeball Juice at Midnight

"**D**o you really think that story was true?" Eric asked Tom on their way out of the store.

"I dunno—but I wouldn't take any chances," Tom said. Eric looked down at his open soda and tucked the packet of Sweet Fizz into his pocket for later.

The four kids made their way over to Thorntree Park and settled at a picnic table under a big maple tree. "I just adore summer!" Nanci said, taking a big drink of her Raspberry Royal.

"Hey, Polly! Hey, Nanci!" called their friends Joan and Blue from just a few tables away. Eric wondered why they were doing homework even though school was out— papers and notebooks were scattered all over their table.

"Hey, you guys, come over here and sit with us," Nanci yelled over. The two girls picked up their things and headed over.

"Great first day of vacation, huh?" Joan asked as she and Blue sat down. Joan had the longest hair of any kid in their school, probably of any kid in the state. It reached down her back, past her waist, all the way down to the backs of her knees.

Her friend Blue had been home-schooled until last year. She was quiet and dressed strangely. Today she was wearing a halter dress with a huge sweater over it. Her sweater was almost as long as Joan's hair.

"What are you guys working on?" Nanci asked, pointing to their notebooks and papers.

"Oh, we've been incredibly busy," said Joan, pulling her long hair over one shoulder. "Blue is helping me get ready for my slumber party. And it's a lot of work."

"Slumber party?" Tom said, making a face. "Yech! Girl stuff!"

Polly glared at him. "Don't worry, Tom, Joan isn't planning to invite you—or any other boys."

"Actually, my mom won't let me have

boys over," Joan said. "But I'd like you to come, Polly, and you too, Nanci."

Polly and Nanci both grinned. "We'd love to come. When is it?" Nanci asked.

"This weekend," Joan said. "That's why Blue and I have so much to do today. We have to buy all the food, rent scary videos, order an ice-cream cake. You know . . ."

Tom and Eric looked at each other. Scary videos sounded like fun. So did a big frosty ice-cream cake.

"Well, Eric," Tom said. "Good thing you're staying over at my house this Saturday. I wouldn't want you to end up drinking eyeball juice at midnight."

"What are you talking about now?" Polly asked, scowling.

"You know," said Eric. "It always happens at slumber parties. Somebody always ends up drinking the eyeball juice by mistake."

Blue surprised everyone by speaking up. "What's eyeball juice?" she asked.

"It sounds gross!" said Nanci.

"I can't believe these girls don't know about eyeball juice," Tom said, looking over at Eric. "I guess we'd better tell them. Remember how my little cousin's best friend's sister in Chicago had to learn about eyeball juice the hard way? . . ."

There was this girl who was having a huge slumber party—she'd invited practically every girl in the seventh grade. She was busy planning the party for weeks, because she wanted everything to be perfect. There would be music and dancing in the living room, a scary video playing in the TV room, and all kinds of snacks in the kitchen.

As soon as her friends started to arrive, the girl knew this was going to be the best slumber party of the year. Everybody brought something along—games, slam books, CDs. And best of all, the girl's parents were away, so the party could go on really late.

After eating their way through all the chips and soda, and dancing to every CD in the house, the girls were ready for a scary movie: *The Slumber Party Massacre*.

It was about a group of girls at a slumber party and a crazy killer who shows up. It was almost too scary to watch, but since the girls were all together, they just huddled close whenever a really gross scene came on. When the movie was over, it was three in the morning, and everybody was ready for bed. The girls spread out their sleeping bags in the den.

One girl realized that she had forgotten the case for her contact lenses. But since she didn't want to bother anyone else, she just got two little paper cups from the bathroom, filled them with water, and put her contacts in them. She set the cups on the coffee table so that no one would knock them over.

Late in the night, another girl woke up thirsty. It was dark in the den, and she couldn't remember which way the bathroom was. She stumbled around for a minute until she ran into the coffee table in the dark. "Ouch!" she whispered. Then she saw two little cups. She picked one up. It was filled with water! She couldn't believe what a great party this was: The hostess had thought of absolutely everything, including a little glass of water for anyone who might be thirsty in the night!

She gulped the water down, but she was still thirsty, so she drank the other cup of water too. She left the empty cups on the table and went back to sleep.

The next morning, everyone woke up very late. It was practically noon by the time the sleeping bags were all rolled up and the girls were ready for breakfast. The girl who had left her contacts on the coffee table went over to put her lenses back in. But when she picked up the little cups, she found that they were empty.

"What happened to my contact lenses?" she asked. "I left them right here in these two little cups."

"Oh no!" said the girl who had woken in the night. "I was thirsty last night. Really thirsty." The girl paused and put her hand on her stomach. "I found those cups on the table, and I thought they were water," she said. "I drank them both!" Suddenly, she felt very, very ill.

Chapter 7

Spider Pus

"That never really happened!" Joan said angrily. "And it's certainly not going to happen at my party! Come on, Blue, we've got more important things to do than sit around here listening to gross stories."

"Suit yourself," Tom said as the two girls walked away. "But remember: Be careful! Watch out for the eyeball juice!" He opened his eyes wide, and then flipped his eyelids inside out—a gross feat he'd perfected in second grade.

Nanci squealed, "Tom! Stop it! Now you're being really disgusting!"

"So immature," Polly hissed, shaking her head.

But Eric didn't have any comment; he was too busy watching the looming shape approaching them. "Uh-oh," he whispered.

Tom flipped his eyelids the right way around just in time to see Johnny Flartt heading their way. The kids all fell silent, watching him approach.

Johnny Flartt was the school bully. He was already twice the size of the other fifth-graders, because he had been kept back twice. Johnny's face was covered with red bumps. Some kids said it was because he was shaving already. Others thought he just had lots and lots of gross pimples.

"Well, well, well. If it isn't my least favorite couple of shrimps and their ugly girl-friends," Johnny said. He plopped down on the bench next to Polly, and she instantly scooted over the other way.

"They aren't our girlfriends," said Tom.

"Oh, yeah?" Johnny said. He reached over and grabbed Polly's Blueberry Freeze. "Hey! How did you know that blueberry was my absolute favorite?" He took a big long slurp.

"That's mine!" Polly said. "Give it back!"

"Really?" Johnny asked. He looked

down at the drink. "That's funny. I could've sworn you got it for me." He took another big drink.

"Give it back to her," Eric said, surprising everyone. Nobody ever stood up to Johnny— not unless they wanted to be squashed like a bug.

"Look at you! Standing up for your little girlfriend!" Johnny laughed. He took another big sip, and then he did something that made Eric really mad. He took the lid off the slushee and dumped the rest of it on the ground. "Oops! Looks like I spilled it. Sorry." He shrugged. "Whaddaya gonna do now, tough guy? Huh? Defend your little girlfriend here?" Johnny sneered at them. He looked really silly, because his lips and teeth were all blue from the blueberry drink.

Tom couldn't help snorting. Then Eric started laughing too.

"What? What's so funny?" Johnny asked. "Tell me what you're laughing about, or I'll cram your teeth down your throat!"

Seeing him try to act tough with those big blue lips made everyone laugh.

"Your lips—they're all blue!" gasped Tom.

"Don't you love Johnny's lipstick?" Nanci asked Polly.

"Yes!" Polly said. "Tell us where you found that *special* shade of blue," she said, and they laughed even harder.

"You're nothing but a bunch of worms!" spat Johnny. As he stood up to leave, he wiped his mouth with the back of his hand, but the blue stain was there to stay.

"Just wait until I get you alone, Camera Boy," Johnny said to Tom. "You're gonna be sorry. And that goes for you, too, you little shrimp!" He pointed at Eric. Then he stormed off, kicking the empty slushee cup out of his way.

"Camera Boy?" Tom said, wiping tears from his eyes. "That's the best he could come up with?"

"I can't stand him," said Polly. "Look at what he did to my slushee!" Pouting, she pointed at the empty cup on the grass.

"Here," Tom said, offering her some of his.

Polly took a sip. Then she said, "Do you

guys know why Johnny had to stay back in third grade?"

"Because he's an idiot?" Tom joked.

"No," said Polly. "It has to do with those red bumps all over his face." She took another sip of Tom's drink.

"Well, are you going to tell us?" Eric asked.

"The way I heard the story," said Polly, "Johnny went on a camping trip with his Cub Scout troop in third grade, and something really horrible happened to him."

"What?" demanded Nanci.

"It was something so terrible that he had to go to the hospital for weeks and weeks. Then when he got back to school, his brain was all messed up. My mom made me promise not to tell anybody," said Polly. "But I guess it's okay to tell you guys."

The third-grade Cub Scout troop had been looking forward to their first camping trip for weeks. But when the troop assembled, carrying sleeping bags, canteens, and back-packs, it was raining. Some of the Scouts grumbled about the weather.

"What are you," demanded the troop leader, "mice or men?"

"*Men!*" shouted the Scouts. Then they put on their ponchos and set off in the downpour.

They reached their campsite by late afternoon, and it was still raining. They pitched their tents and tried to light a campfire, but the wood was too wet to burn. By now all the boys were miserable, and so was their leader. "What do you say we call it a day, boys?" he said. "Tomorrow this will clear up, and we'll go on a hike." The boys all agreed. They crawled into their damp tents and started to get ready for bed.

In one tent there was this big, mean kid who was always roughhousing and getting into trouble. He was known to pull practical jokes a lot too. And sure enough, just as everyone was falling asleep, he yelled, "*Help! There's a snake in my sleeping bag!*" Everyone came running to his tent, only to find him sitting there laughing.

"Ha-ha! Fooled you! There aren't any

snakes in these woods, you big babies."

No one thought his joke was very funny, especially since they'd run out in the rain in their pajamas to help him. When they were back in their tent, two of the other Scouts got an idea. What if they really did put something gross in the mean kid's sleeping bag? If they couldn't get a snake, how about a big fat juicy spider?

So the two boys went out into the rainy night with their flashlights and turned over rocks and branches until they found a spider. It wasn't very big, but it would do.

They crept up to the bully's tent and slipped the spider inside. "I hope it bites him all over!" one of the boys whispered. "Me too!" agreed the other one.

The next day, the rain clouds broke up and the sun came out. Everyone, including the troop leader, was in a better mood on the hike back home. When they stopped for lunch, the leader congratulated all the boys for keeping their spirits up despite the bad weather.

As they sat around the campfire cooking hot dogs, the troop leader noticed something on the bully's face. "What's that red bump on your cheek?" he asked.

The bully reached up and felt his face. "I dunno. . . ."

One of the other boys said, "It's a big fat zit!" and everyone laughed.

"Shut up, or I'll smash you like bugs!" snarled the bully, shaking his fist.

"That's enough of that! Pipe down!" snapped the troop leader. The boys quieted down, and the whole thing was forgotten by the time they'd finished their hot dogs.

When the bully got home later that day, his mom also noticed the bump on his face. "What's that red bump? Is it a pimple?" she asked him.

"I dunno," said the bully. "Leave me alone."

By the next day, the bump was bigger and redder. And now it itched, too. When the bully's mother saw it, she said, "I think a dermatologist should look at that."

"Just leave me alone!" said the bully. He didn't like having pimples, and this one was really getting on his nerves. By that evening it had grown even bigger, and it was itching like crazy.

"Maybe it's not a pimple," his mother said. "Maybe it's a bug bite. Did a bug bite you on your camping trip?"

"I dunno," the bully said. "Leave me alone."

By the next day, the bully couldn't ignore the red bump any longer. It was huge, his whole face was swollen, and it itched so badly that he couldn't stop scratching it.

"I'm taking you to the doctor," his mother said. She called the dermatologist, who said she'd see the boy right away.

"My goodness!" she exclaimed as she examined the huge red sore. "What happened to you?"

"I dunno," the bully said.

"This may be a pimple or a bug bite," said the doctor, "but either way, I'll have to cut it open to stop the swelling." She prepared a scalpel and rubbed the bump with alcohol.

"*Ouch!*" shouted the bully. "That hurts!"

"This will only take a second," the doctor

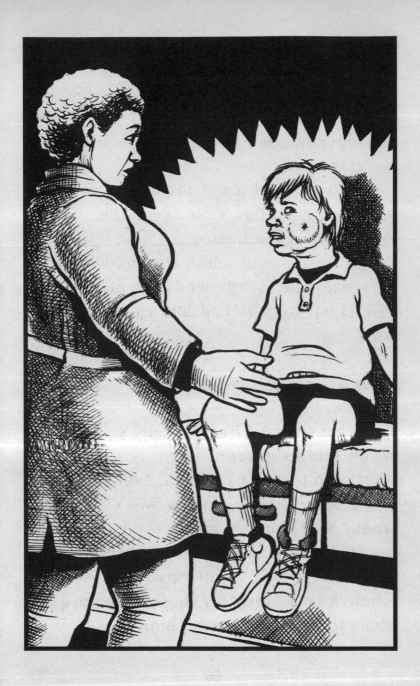

said. But as she pressed the scalpel into the sore, thousands of little black things came swarming out of the bump.

"*AAAAAHHHHH!*" screamed the doctor, backing away. Baby spiders were streaming out of the cut!

"What? What is it?" the bully asked. But the doctor couldn't answer—she simply closed her eyes in horror.

It turned out that the spider those boys had put in the bully's tent had not only bitten him, it had laid eggs under his skin! . . .

"Wait a second," Eric said. "That happened to *Johnny*?"

"That's what I heard," Polly said, finishing off Tom's slushee.

"I don't think I believe it," said Tom.

"I don't believe Johnny was ever a Cub Scout," said Nanci. "I mean, *really*."

"I'm just telling you what I heard," Polly said. "And if you want proof, just look at Johnny's face—they say those red bumps are where the baby spiders bit him!"

"Eeewwwwwwww!" the kids all said at once.

"Whether it happened to Johnny or not, that's the creepiest story I've ever heard," said Eric.

"Make that the creepy-*crawliest* story!" said Tom.

Chapter 8

The Sleepy Fruit Vendor and the Dancing Cactus

"**W**ell, whatever made Johnny so mean, I hope we don't have to see much more of him this summer," said Nanci.

"I agree," said Tom. "What are you guys doing for the rest of the day?"

"Don't know. I guess we could head back to the pool," said Nanci.

"We've already missed the peak sun hours. Let's do something else," said Polly.

"Want to go see that new movie at the multiplex?" asked Tom.

"Yeah!" Nanci said instantly. "Great idea!"

"Is that the one about the slimy sea creature? I'm not sure I want to see it. I heard it's really, really gross," said Polly.

"Come on! It'll be fun if we all go," said Tom.

"I can't," Eric said. "I'm supposed to run a bunch of errands for my mom, and it's already two o'clock."

"Can't you do them tomorrow?" Tom asked. Eric shook his head. He knew his mother needed all the ingredients for her secret pasta sauce tonight. She was counting on him to do the grocery shopping.

"Let's head over to the movie theater and see what time the next show starts," Nanci suggested. "Maybe we can get Eric to change his mind on the way."

As they left the park, they passed a vendor who was selling bananas, grapes, apples, and plums from a little cart. "Wait up, you guys," Nanci said. "I want to get some grapes to eat at the movies."

Polly grabbed Nanci's arm and dragged her away from the cart. "Don't buy those!" she whispered. "You'll end up like the sleepy fruit vendor!"

"What are you talking about?" asked Eric.

"You know—the guy who was selling bananas and kept falling asleep at his fruit stand," said Polly.

"Maybe he was tired," Tom said, laughing.

"It's not a joke!" said Polly. "My mom told me never to buy fruit from a stand, because they don't wash it. You never know what's on it."

"What does that have to do with the sleepy fruit guy?" asked Eric.

"Everything," Polly answered. "My mom told me this story, and she heard it from our postman, so I know it's true. . . ."

There used to be a fruit stand on the corner of Maple and Main streets. The guy who worked there was always bragging that his fruit was the freshest in town. When he got deliveries, he would unpack the crates immediately and start selling the fruit right away.

One day he got in a huge crate of bananas from Mexico. He unpacked it quickly, stacking all the fresh yellow fruit in a big pyramid. Then he turned the crate over and stood on it, calling out, "Fresh bananas! Come and get your fresh bananas here! Straight from Mexico to you!"

A lot of people came by, and no one could

resist the bananas; they looked so good. After a while, the fruit vendor got tired of shouting, so he sat down on the crate. The bananas were selling quickly, but suddenly the vendor was so sleepy, he could hardly make change. He didn't know what was wrong with him— it was barely past noon, and he couldn't seem to keep his eyes open. Then he got so sleepy that he toppled off the crate and crashed to the ground. Some customers tried to wake him up, but it was no use. It was as if he was in a coma. They called an ambulance.

When the ambulance arrived, the fruit vendor was still in a very deep sleep. Just then, a man walked up to the fruit stand carrying a bunch of bananas in a plastic bag. In his other hand he held a glass jar. "What happened here?" he asked.

"The fruit vendor just passed out," answered someone in the crowd.

"The same thing happened to my son when he tried to eat one of these bananas," said the man.

"What do you mean?" asked the ambulance driver.

"My son was fine one minute. The next thing we knew, he had passed out with a banana in his hand. We looked through the bunch of bananas and found this." The man held out the glass jar. Inside was a huge, hairy tarantula!

The ambulance attendant started searching through the bananas on the cart, and sure enough, he found a whole nest of tarantulas! They'd crawled into the crate in Mexico, along with the bananas. And when the fruit vendor was unpacking the crate, they'd bitten him. . . .

"That sounds just like the story you told us about Johnny and the spider," said Nanci. "Are you sure it's true?"

"Definitely," said Polly. "You guys know I wouldn't make it up."

"I believe it," Eric said, "'cause once I heard a story just like that from my cousin's best friend in North Carolina. He said . . ."

There was this guy who had just started college. He was living in a dorm room with a roommate, and they didn't have much furniture, just two beds and a desk. So they decided to get some things to liven up the room—posters, a beanbag chair, that kind of stuff.

They went to the biggest department store in the neighborhood and started shopping. They got a rug, a small bookshelf, and two posters. Then one of the guys noticed this cool cactus. It was in a big clay pot, and it was really big, almost as tall as he was. "This would look so cool in our dorm room," he said to his roommate. They agreed that they had to get it.

When they carried it to the cashier, she said, "That's the last one of those we've got. They've been selling like crazy since we got the shipment in from Mexico."

"So this is a real Mexican cactus?" the guy asked her.

"Yep. I helped unpack the boxes myself. Straight from Mexico," she said.

When they got back to the dorm, the guys spent the rest of the afternoon fixing up their room. It looked pretty good when they got done, but the best part about their redecorating job was the cactus. It sat in a corner by the window, and everyone who came by the room commented on how cool it was.

Early that evening, while they were studying in their newly refurbished dorm room, one of the guys thought he heard a strange noise. "What's that humming sound?" he asked his roommate.

"I don't know, but I've been hearing it too," his roommate replied.

They kept studying, but the humming grew louder. "What *is* that noise? It's driving me nuts!" said one of them.

"Me too," said the other. "I can hardly study."

"Sounds like it's coming from over by the window." The first guy got up to investigate and ended up standing right next to their new cactus.

"It's insane, but I think the noise is coming from the cactus!" he said.

His roommate came over and listened. "You're right," he said. "And look at it! Is it moving, or am I crazy?"

The cactus did seem to be moving, swaying ever so slightly from side to side.

"This is too weird. I'm calling the store where we bought it." He picked up the phone, dialed, and asked for the manager. He felt a little silly explaining the problem.

"Where's the cactus now?" asked the store manager.

"I'm standing right next to it."

"Get out of there! *Hurry!*" screamed the manager.

"Why?" The guy was completely puzzled.

"Get outside! We'll send help. Just get out *now!*"

So the guys ran out of their room, even though they didn't understand what was going on. By the time they reached the front door of the dormitory, a big white truck was pulling up. Two men dressed in spacesuits stepped out. They wore all kinds of protective gear, including big helmets with glass faceplates.

"Where's the cactus?" asked one of them.

The guy told them their room number, and the two men disappeared inside the building. They appeared a few minutes later, carrying the cactus between them.

"Step back!" one of the men ordered. "Stay away from the cactus!"

The two roommates backed up. By now

they could see that the cactus was definitely moving, rocking back and forth in its pot as if it was alive.

Then one of the men said, "Look out! I think it's gonna blow!" And sure enough, the cactus exploded. It burst open with a loud crunching noise, and a swarming black cloud settled over the campus walk—and the two men. They screamed, dropped the pot, and tried frantically to brush away the black things that were crawling all over them.

The roommates could hardly believe what they were seeing: Hundreds of big, fat, hairy tarantulas had burst out of the cactus, and now they were heading straight for the dormitory! . . .

"Eric, just because you know *another* bizarre story about tarantulas doesn't make Polly's story true," Tom said.

"Yeah, I think you guys are just really scared of spiders," Nanci said. "And I still don't believe that tarantulas could live in a cactus—*or* in a bunch of bananas!"

"Fine," Eric said. "I don't care if you

believe it or not. I know it's true. But maybe you'll have to learn the hard way. . . ." Eric's hand crawled up Nanci's back like a spider.

"That's not funny!" Nanci said, pushing him away. "Here's the grocery store. Didn't you say you had to go shopping?"

"Yeah," Eric admitted. "I do. You guys have fun at the movies."

"I'm sure we will—especially if we don't have to hear any more spider stories!" said Polly.

"Careful with the bananas," called Tom as Eric headed into the supermarket.

Chapter 9

Casserole à la Corpse

Eric fished his mom's list out of his pocket and headed toward the produce section.

Lettuce, he read, and put a head of lettuce into the shopping cart. *Carrots*. He dropped in a big bag of carrots. *Green apples*. He picked up some apples from the bin and dropped them into the cart too.

Eric didn't mind doing the grocery shopping. Actually, he thought it was kind of fun. His parents trusted him with the money to buy groceries for the whole week, which was a pretty big deal. They would never trust Shawn with that.

The only problem with shopping was that sometimes Eric got confused and brought home the wrong things. Once his mom had written *green peppers* on the list, and the only green peppers he could find were jalapeños. How was he supposed to know that jalapeños are practically the hottest green peppers in the world?

After that, Eric was especially careful. If there was something on the list that he didn't recognize, he asked someone in the store to help him.

"Pasta," Eric said, putting two boxes of spaghetti into the cart. "Tarragon. Tarragon? What's that?" Was it a fruit? A vegetable? Or something else? Eric decided to ask a stock boy.

"Excuse me," he said. "Can you tell me where to find tarragon?"

"Sure," said the stock boy, whose name tag read ROB. "Aisle five, with the rest of the herbs and spices."

"Oh," Eric said. "Tarragon's a spice?"

"Nope, it's an herb. Do you need me to help you find it?"

"Sure," Eric said. "I've never seen it before."

"Follow me," said Rob. He led Eric past the candy and soda aisle to an area where rows and rows of little glass jars lined the shelves.

"Here's the tarragon," said Rob, handing Eric a jar.

"Boy, there sure are a lot of spices here." Eric couldn't believe that he'd never noticed this section of the supermarket before. It was really big. He'd never heard of half these things, either.

"Yup, we have all the spices in the world at FoodMart," said Rob. "Well, *almost*."

"Which ones don't you have?" asked Eric.

"We don't have any Accidental Cannibal spice." Rob smiled.

"Accidental Cannibal spice? What's that?"

"It's quite a delicacy over in Europe," said Rob. "I'll tell you why. . . ."

There was this man from Italy who lived in New York City. He was the only member of his family who had left the homeland, and he was lonely in America. His family back in Italy missed him too. But as the years went by, they thought of him less and less, until he was almost forgotten.

By his old age, the man had grown rich. His business—he imported Italian spices—had done very well. Because he never married, and he didn't have many American friends, the man left his entire fortune to his family back in Italy.

Shortly after he made out his will, the man died. He'd left instructions for his body to be cremated, and for the ashes to be shipped home to Italy in a beautiful urn. In settling the estate, the man's lawyer sent a check to the family in Italy with a note explaining that their long-lost cousin had passed away and left them everything. But the lawyer didn't speak Italian, so he wrote the letter in English.

When the family in Italy got the letter and the check, they didn't understand that the man was dead. They saw their cousin's name on the check, and guessed that he was sending them money because he was so generous and so successful in America. They took the money and sent back a thank-you note.

When the man's lawyer got the thank-you note, he couldn't read it because it was in Italian. But he figured it must be a nice note, since it was written on such pretty paper. Now that he had contacted the man's family, the lawyer had to do one last thing: He had to send the man's ashes back to his homeland.

So the lawyer packed up the urn with great care and sent it to the family in Italy. When the Italian family received the beautiful urn from America, they knew it must be another gift from their generous cousin. But what was it? Then they remembered how their cousin had earned his fortune: He'd owned a spice company. The strange powder in the urn must be some wonderful, exotic spice.

That night at dinner, everyone sprinkled a little of the powder on their food. It was so good! The powder made everything taste better. How clever their cousin was—no wonder he was so rich! It wasn't long before the family was putting the special spice on all their meals—lunch, dinner, even breakfast. After a few weeks, the urn was half empty. The family loved the special powder so much

that they didn't want to go without it for even a day. So they wrote to their cousin in America, telling him how much they loved the special spice and asking him for more of it.

When the American lawyer received the family's letter, he was puzzled. Why were they writing? He wanted to make sure that they had received the urn with the old man's ashes, so he decided to find someone who could translate the letter.

When the translator told him what the letter said, the lawyer almost passed out.

Thank you so much for sending us your tasty new spice powder. We love it so much, we put it on everything we eat. But the beautiful urn you sent us is almost empty. Can we please have some more of this delicious spice? Your loving family . . .

"Ewwww," Eric said. "You mean they were eating the dead guy's ashes? That's so gross!"

"I know," said Rob. "But hey, it was an honest mistake. I mean, look at all these jars. Who knows what's really in 'em?"

Eric looked down at the jar in his hand.

"So what's in tarragon, anyway?" he asked.

"I dunno. Tarragon, I guess."

"But what *is* tarragon?" Eric asked.

"Beats me!" said Rob, grinning.

Chapter 10

One Large Rat Juice, to Go!

Carrying a grocery bag on each arm, Eric trudged down the sidewalk in the sunshine. He could hardly believe the first day of vacation was so hot. Tomorrow he would definitely get to his swimming lesson at ten so that he could stay in the pool for a good long time.

As he passed the video store, Eric heard someone call his name. For a second, he thought it might be Johnny Flartt. To his relief, it wasn't—it was his friend Kevin, coming out of the store.

"Hey," said Eric. "What's up?"

"Not much. What's in those bags?" Kevin asked.

"Groceries," Eric answered. "I do the grocery shopping for the family," he added proudly.

"Really?" Kevin said. "Sounds tough."

"It's okay," Eric said. "My parents give me the money, and I get to keep any change that's left over."

"Well, *that's* cool. Did you have any change today?" Kevin asked.

Eric put down a bag and searched around in his pocket. "Seventy-nine cents," he said.

"Wanna go get a soda?" Kevin asked.

"Okay, but I have to be home soon—if I don't put this ice cream in the freezer, it's gonna melt all over the place."

"Then I'll help you carry this stuff home," Kevin offered.

"Hey, thanks." Eric had always liked Kevin, even though Tom didn't. Tom thought Kevin was nerdy because he didn't talk much. But Eric liked to play chess with Kevin. He was a good chess partner because he was quiet. Tom was *never* quiet.

As if Kevin had read Eric's mind, he asked, "You gonna play any chess this summer?"

"Yeah," Eric said. "My dad just got a new computer that has an excellent program on it—master-level games and stuff like that."

"Cool," Kevin said. He picked up one of the grocery bags.

"Hey, let's get sodas from the machine outside the hardware store," said Eric. "That's on the way to my house."

"No way." Kevin shook his head. "I never drink soda from machines."

"Why not?"

"You know—the mouse in the soda bottle."

"Huh?" Eric asked. "What mouse?"

"Well, one time this kid told me about a friend of his," said Kevin. "He got a bottle of soda from a machine . . ."

It was a hot summer day, and this kid was dying for a cold drink. So he put his change in the machine, got out a cola, and took a big long gulp. The first swallow tasted okay, but the next one had a funny aftertaste.

He took another sip, which tasted even worse. "One last sip," he decided, because he was so thirsty. But when he tipped the bottle up to his lips he thought he saw something

floating around inside. He spat out what was in his mouth, and emptied the bottle on the sidewalk.

As the soda poured out, he could see something in the bottle—something small and dark. He held the bottle up and got the shock of his life. Inside was a dead mouse— and it was all rotted away in spots, so you could even see its tiny skeleton!

The kid started throwing up all over the street, and eventually they had to take him to the hospital. Nobody ever figured out how the mouse got in there, but it must've been at the factory.

"Yuck! That's so gross!" Eric said.

"I know," Kevin replied. "That's why I only buy a soda that I can inspect first, like at a store. When you get it out of a machine, who knows what might be in it?"

As they walked past the convenience store, Kevin said, "Wanna get a soda in here?"

"Naw," Eric said. "I'm not that thirsty anymore."

"Well, I'm gonna go. I'm so thirsty, I could drink a rat juice!" Kevin said, handing over the groceries. "I'll see you around later this summer, maybe."

"Yeah, maybe," Eric said. Kevin might not talk very much, thought Eric, but when he did, he sure came up with some weird stuff.

Chapter 11

The Viper Belly Dance

As Eric walked up the driveway, he realized that he'd forgotten to pick up more Fudge-Os at the grocery store. Shawn was going to be mad about that.

He let himself into the house and went to the kitchen to unpack the groceries. Shawn was sitting at the table. He didn't even look up from his magazine when Eric came in.

"Hey. When's Dad getting home?"

"Don't know and don't care," snarled Shawn.

"What's got you in such a bad mood?" Eric asked.

"Maybe living with you for the past fifteen years," Shawn said.

"You haven't lived with me for fifteen years, because I'm only eleven," Eric pointed out. "You *are* fifteen years old, but you had the first four years to yourself. Which is more than *I* had," he added under his breath.

Shawn glared at him. "Oh, just shut up."

"What is your major malfunction? You've been really mean to me all day."

Shawn let out a heavy sigh. "You know how I failed biology this year? Well, I just found out that Mom and Dad are sending me to some dorky science camp this summer to make up the credits." Shawn threw his magazine down on the table and leaned back in his chair. "Two months in the middle of nowhere with a bunch of science geeks? Not exactly my idea of a good summer."

"That really doesn't sound good," said Eric. "Where's the camp?"

"Who knows?" Shawn said. "Somewhere between here and the middle of nowhere. What difference does it make, anyhow?"

"It *does* make a difference. Camp can be dangerous," said Eric. "Lemme give you some advice: If they make you go out hiking, don't fill up your canteen in any streams or rivers."

"Why not?" Shawn asked.

"Remember Damon, from my soccer

team? He told me about this one kid who got sent away to camp . . ."

There was this city kid who got sent to a camp way off in the country. At first, all the hiking and swimming bored him. But after a couple of weeks, he started to like the quiet of the woods and being around nature. Then he got to be friends with another kid in his bunk, and he really started to have a good time.

One day when all the other kids were at free swim, the city kid and his friend decided to go for a hike in the woods. They took off without telling anybody where they were going—they figured they'd only be gone for a few hours. But after hiking for the whole afternoon, the two boys couldn't find their way back to camp. They walked and walked, but nothing looked familiar.

As the sun started to go down, they looked for some shelter, and finally they decided to sleep under a big tree. It was hard to get comfortable; they were hungry and cold, and they kept hearing strange noises in the dark. But they curled up and tried to rest. And just as soon as the morning sun started to peek through the branches, they were up again, looking for the camp. They must've wandered around for hours with nothing to eat or drink before they finally found a little stream.

"I'm so thirsty!" the city kid said. He started filling his empty canteen in the stream.

"Me too," said his friend, wading into the water. "This water feels great! It's so nice and cold and . . . *argh!*" he yelled suddenly. The city kid scrambled over and saw what his friend was hollering about. There, at the bottom of the stream, was a huge snake! Both boys ran out of the water and stood panting on the bank.

"I've never seen such a big snake! And did you see its babies?"

"Babies?" the city kid asked.

"Yeah, a whole nest of 'em. Come on, let's get out of here!"

The two boys walked and walked, with only the one canteen to share between them.

When the water was almost all gone, the city kid said, "I get the last sip, because it's my canteen."

"That's not fair!" said his friend. "You've been hogging that canteen all morning. And I'm really thirsty!"

"Too bad," the city kid said. "It's my canteen, so I get the last drink." And with that, he drank every last drop in the canteen. But just as he finished, he half gagged, half choked. *"Haauck!"* he coughed, spitting some of the water back up. "I think I just swallowed something weird."

"Like I care," said his friend.

Just then, the boys heard someone in the distance calling out to them. It was one of the camp counselors. They were finally found.

The two boys became camp heroes thanks to their adventure. But they didn't have much time to enjoy it; camp was just about over.

When the city kid's mom came to pick him up, she thought he looked different. "What did they do to you here?" she asked. "I've never seen you so skinny." The kid shrugged. He'd been eating as much as always. His mom was just imagining things.

But once they were back at home, the kid got thinner and thinner. Finally his mom was so worried, she took him to the doctor. The doctor examined the kid and couldn't find anything wrong.

"But I *know* he's losing weight," his mother said. The kid had to agree. He'd lost a few pounds, but he didn't know why.

"Make sure he eats three healthy meals a day," the doctor told her. "I'm sure that will solve the problem." And he showed them out.

But as the weeks went by, the kid kept getting thinner and thinner. They went back to the doctor, and now it was obvious to everyone that something was wrong. "Young man, you've lost almost ten pounds since you were last here," said the doctor. "What seems to be the problem?"

The kid was baffled. "I'm eating a lot—more than ever—but I'm hungry all the time," he said. "I don't know what's going on."

So the doctor decided to run a few tests. He took some blood from the kid's arm. "I'm going to take an X ray, too, just to be sure," he said.

The kid and his mom were in the waiting room when the doctor rushed in. "We have to perform emergency surgery, *now*!" he cried.

"Why? What's wrong?" the mother asked.

But the nurses were already wheeling her son away on a gurney, into the operating room. The mother ran after them and watched as they quickly put her son to sleep and cut open his stomach.

"Nurse! Hand me that specimen jar!" barked the doctor.

"I don't think it will be big enough, doctor," said the nurse, retching. The doctor ignored her and reached down into the kid's stomach.

The mother almost passed out when she saw what had been living inside her son: a four-foot-long snake! It must have gotten into him when he drank the stream water

from his canteen weeks before. It was only a baby then. But it had been living—and growing—in his stomach ever since!

"Oh, man!" said Shawn. "Is that true?"

"That's what Damon told me. And he actually knows the kid's friend."

Shawn shook his head. "I didn't wanna go to camp before I heard that story," he said. "Now I *really* don't wanna go."

"Maybe you should study harder next year," said Eric. "And drink bottled water this summer!"

Shawn just scowled. "Very funny, little bro. Very funny."

Chapter 12

Return of the Chicken-Fried Rat

"**I**'m home!" called Eric's dad. "Where is everybody?"

Eric came out of the den to find his dad in the kitchen. "Hi, Dad," he said.

"Hey, kiddo," said his father, opening the refrigerator. "I see you did the grocery shopping. Thanks. How was your first day of summer vacation?"

"Okay." Then Eric thought about it for a minute. "Actually, it was pretty awful," he finally said.

"Awful? Why?"

"Well, first I found this gross thing in my cereal, then I was late to my swimming lesson, and I didn't even get to go to the movies!" The more Eric thought about it, the more awful the day seemed. Except for one thing . . .

"Are you guys really sending Shawn away to camp?" he asked.

His father sighed. "Shawn just isn't working hard enough at school. This is the only thing we could do. I know you may be lonely this summer without him, but you could invite Tom over more often to keep you company."

"That sounds great!" Eric said. Things were looking better already.

"And I have something else that will cheer you up," Dad said. "Your mom can't cook tonight. She's going to be late. So I picked up a little something for dinner on my way home—something you're really going to like."

"What is it?" asked Eric.

"Your favorite," his dad said. "Fried chicken!"

A vision of the deep-fried rat Shawn had told him about flashed into Eric's head. "Ugh!" he exclaimed.

"What do you mean, 'ugh'? I thought you loved fried chicken."

"You're right," Eric said, trying to think

of an excuse. "It's just that I . . . uh . . . have a lot of homework to do tonight. Actually, I have so much homework, I better get started on it right now."

"Homework? On the first day of vacation? I've never heard of such a thing."

"Middle school is really tough now," Eric called out as he raced up the stairs.

"Should I save a drumstick for you in case you get hungry later?" his father called after him.

Eric thought for a second. "No, thanks," he called down, grinning. "Give it to Shawn. He loves chicken-fried ra—I mean chicken."

If you liked

The Chicken-Fried RAT

you won't want to miss . . .

Feel like
a good laugh?

You will when you read about . . .

    * The guy who flushed a toilet—
       and made it explode!

    * The lady who got rich from using the
       restroom at a funeral parlor.

    * The cops who tricked a criminal into
confessing—to a photocopying machine.

Are these stories for real—
or are they just too funny
to be true?

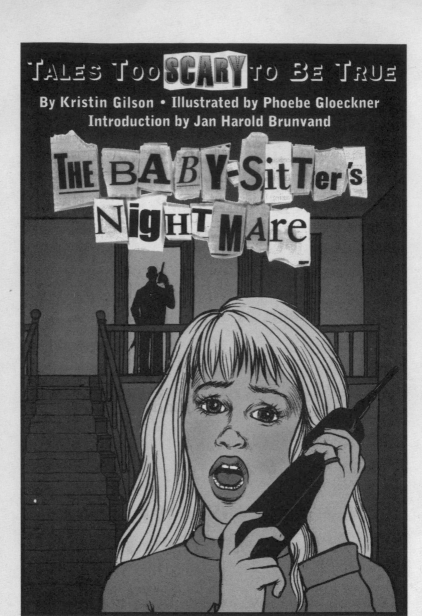